DRAGON in THE WOOD

BY LUCY KINCAID
ILLUSTRATED BY ERIC KINCAID

BRIMAX BOOKS · NEWMARKET · ENGLAND

It is a hot day.
The birds are asleep.
The bees are asleep.
The rabbits are asleep.
All the animals are asleep.
Only the flowers are awake.

The birds wake up.
The bees wake up.
The rabbits wake up.
All the animals wake up.
"What is that?" they say.

"Who is coming?" say the birds
"Who is coming?" say the animals.
"It is a dragon," say the bees.
The animals are afraid.
They all hide.
The flowers do not hide.

They all look at the
dragon.
The dragon is hot.
He sits down.
They can all see the
dragon.
The dragon cannot see
them.
They are hiding.

What will the dragon do?
The dragon shuts his eyes.
The dragon opens his
mouth.
The dragon begins to sing.
They do not like the
dragon's song.
They all want him to stop
singing.

They all come out of
hiding.
"Stop!" say the birds.
"Stop!" say the bees.
"Stop!" say all the
animals.
The dragon stops singing.

The dragon opens his eyes.
"Where have you come
from?" says the dragon.
"We live here," say the
birds.
"I did not see you," says
the dragon.
"We were all hiding," say
the bees.

"Can I sing a song for you?" says the dragon.
"No! No! Please do not sing," they say.
The dragon looks sad.
"Nobody will let me sing," he says.
The dragon begins to cry.
They have never seen a dragon cry.

"Are you a real dragon?"
they say.
The dragon shows them
that he is.
He puffs smoke.
He spits fire.
They are all afraid.
They all run away.
"Come back," says the
dragon. "I will not hurt
you. I just want to sing."

"We will help you," say the birds. "Listen to us."
The dragon listens to the birds.
The dragon opens his mouth. He tries to sing like the birds. He cannot. He puffs smoke. He spits fire.
"Stop!" say the birds.
"Stop!" say the bees.
"Stop!" say the animals.

The dragon is sad. He walks away.

"Come back!" say the animals.

"We will help you," say the bees.

"How?" say the birds.

"Bees cannot sing."

"We can hum," say the bees.

"Humming is like singing."

The bees begin to hum.

"Can I do that?" says the dragon.
"You can if you try," say the bees.
The dragon tries to hum. He can do it. He can hum just like the bees. "Hum hum hum," hums the dragon.
Nobody tells him to stop. "Hum hum hum," says the dragon.

Dragon is humming a
song.
The bees are humming too.
The birds are singing.
The animals join in.
The rabbits tap their feet.
The flowers nod their
heads.
They are all happy.

Say these words again

listen	spits
mouth	their
asleep	join
animals	nobody
hiding	singing
afraid	hurt
humming	flowers